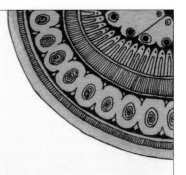

The WOODCUTTER
and the
MOST BEAUTIFUL TREE

Robb N. Johnston

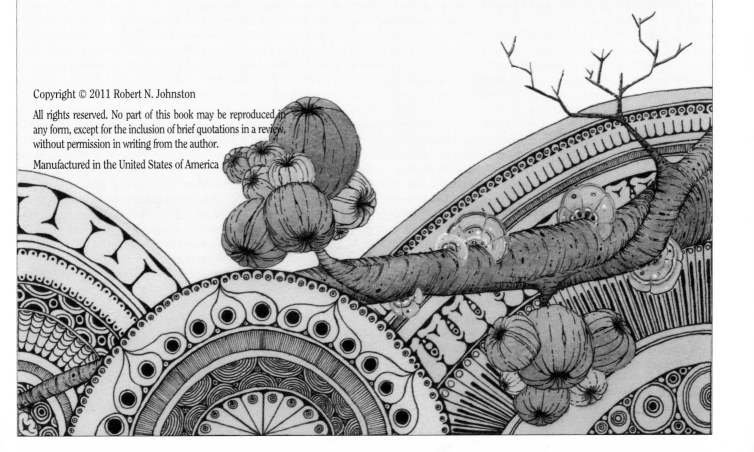

It was springtime…and the woodcutter sang to himself as he tromped through the cool, bright forest:

Suddenly, he came upon The Most Beautiful Tree.

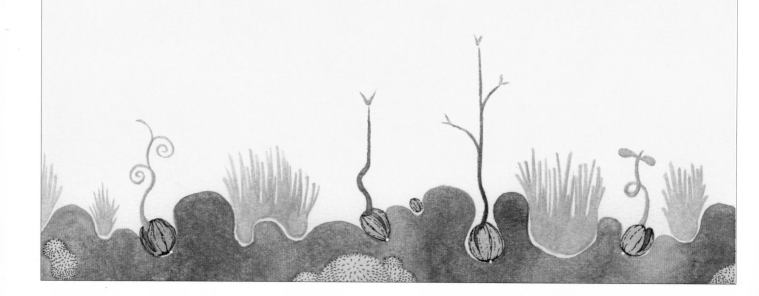

He lifted his axe to take the first, mighty swing…
and the tree spoke!

"Excuse me," she said, "what are you doing?"

The woodcutter answered, "I will CHOP-CHOP-CHOP you
DOWN-DOWN-DOWN!"

"Oh, I see," said the tree. "Carry on, then. Still, it seems like
such a waste, what with me being in full bloom this time of
year."

"Hmm...you DO have incredible flowers," said the woodcutter as he looked at her colorful blossoms.

"Why, thank you!" said the tree, ruffling herself to make her flowers look all the more amazing. "Won't you take some home to your wife?"

The woodcutter thought about this...

...then, he did.

The woodcutter panted and puffed as he
crashed through the hot, summer forest:

It wasn't long before he happened upon The Most Beautiful Tree.

He lifted his axe to take the first, mighty swing... and the tree spoke!

"Ah, hello again," said the tree rather lazily. "Did you come back to thank me for the flowers?"

The woodcutter hefted his axe, "I came to CHOP-CHOP-CHOP you DOWN-DOWN-DOWN!"

"Oh, I see," yawned the tree, "by all means."

"And yet, it seems such a shame to be chopping and sweating on a hot summer day, ESPECIALLY when my leaves are providing such cool shade."

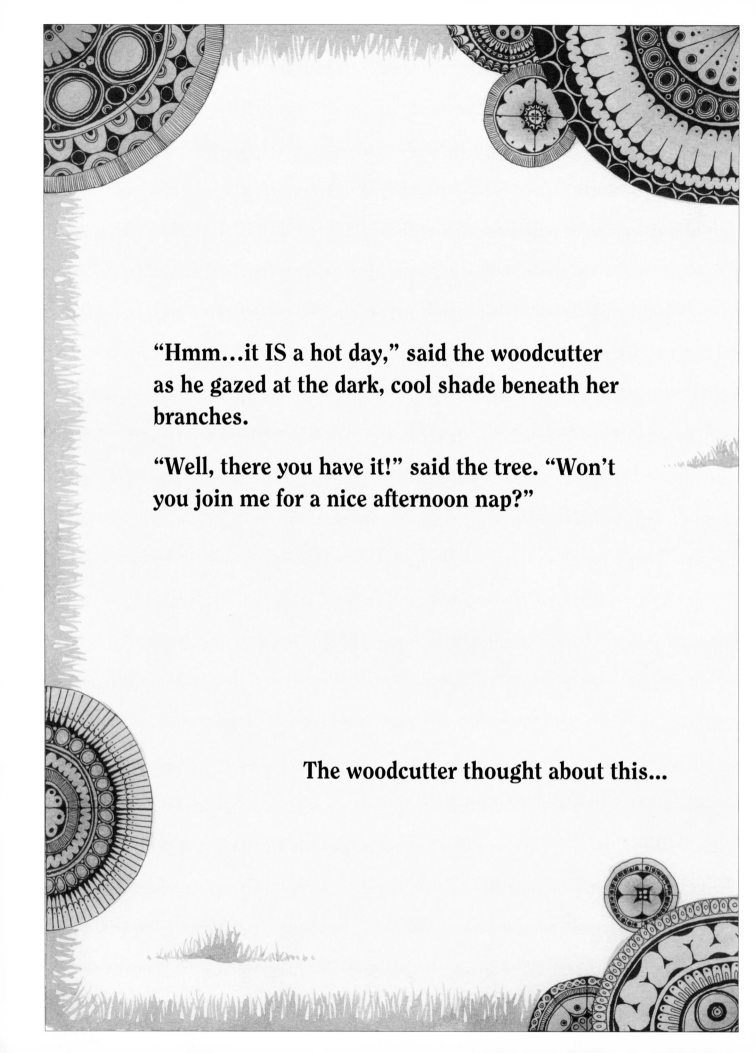

"Hmm...it IS a hot day," said the woodcutter as he gazed at the dark, cool shade beneath her branches.

"Well, there you have it!" said the tree. "Won't you join me for a nice afternoon nap?"

The woodcutter thought about this...

...then, he did.

Leaves crunched & crackled under the woodcutter's feet as he strode through the brisk, autumn woods singing:

Sure enough, he found The Most Beautiful Tree looking just as glorious as ever. Once more, he readied his axe to take the first, mighty swing…and the tree spoke!

"Hello there," she gasped, "have you come by for another nap?"

The woodcutter gripped the cold axe in his thick hands. "I came to CHOP-CHOP-CHOP you DOWN-DOWN-DOWN!"

"Oh, I see," grunted the tree, "as you will. But first, would you help me get rid of these heavy, heavy nuts? I've been holding them in my branches all season long and I'm getting so very tired. Maybe you would even have use for them?" she asked.

"Hmm...my wife DOES make excellent nut pancakes," said the woodcutter as he gazed at the bounty on the tree's creaking limbs.

"I'm sure she does!" came the reply as a gentle breeze dropped some nuts onto the forest floor. "Please take as many as you like."

The woodcutter thought about this...

...then, he did.

All was quiet as the woodcutter slowly made his way through the cold winter forest.

-

After a long time, he found The Most Beautiful Tree…

although these days, she did not feel very beautiful.

"Oh, hello again," she sighed. "I suppose you're here to chop-chop-chop me down-down-down."

The woodcutter only looked at her.

"I don't have any beautiful flowers," she said.

"I can see that," said the woodcutter.

"Nor do I have any leaves to shade you," she continued.

"It's too cold to nap in the shade," he replied.

"I don't even have any nuts or seeds for you to collect," she whispered.

"You gave me more than enough to last the long winter," said the woodcutter.

The tree took a deep breath

and looked away as the woodcutter
approached her.

But when the tree finally looked at herself,
she couldn't believe what she saw!

She was wrapped in a delicate garland,
almost as splendid as her spring flowers.

Her branches were hung with ornaments made of crystal, gold, and silver. When the cold winter light touched her ornaments, the tree cast a soft, warm glow throughout the entire forest.

"MERRY CHRISTMAS!"

Bellowed the woodcutter as he wrapped his thick arms around the trunk of The Most Beautiful Tree.

He hugged her and gave her a big, bristly kiss from his big, bristly face.

The tree blushed, feeling more beautiful than ever.

"You have a merry Christmas, too!" she gushed.

The woodcutter thought about this...

...then,

he did.